Praise for Peter Brandvold and his Western novels

"Make room on your shelf of favorites; Peter Brandvold will be staking out a claim there."   —Frank Roderus

"Peter Brandvold will be the next Louis L'Amour."
                    —Rosanne Bittner, author of *Follow Your Heart*

"A natural born storyteller who knows the West as well as any of those writing in the genre today."
                    —Bill Brooks, author of the *Dakota Lawman* series

"An action-packed, entertaining read for fans of traditional Westerns."   —*Booklist* on *Dakota Kill*

"Brandvold is a writer to watch."
                    —Jory Sherman, author of *The Vigilante*

"Recommended to anyone who loves the West as I do. A very good read."   —Jack Ballas, author of *Gun Boss*

HELL ON WHEELS

PETER BRANDVOLD

BERKLEY BOOKS, NEW YORK

THE BERKLEY PUBLISHING GROUP
Published by the Penguin Group
Penguin Group (USA) Inc.
375 Hudson Street, New York, New York 10014, USA
Penguin Group (Canada), 90 Eglinton Avenue East, Suite 700, Toronto, Ontario M4P 2Y3, Canada
(a division of Pearson Penguin Canada Inc.)
Penguin Books Ltd., 80 Strand, London WC2R 0RL, England
Penguin Group Ireland, 25 St. Stephen's Green, Dublin 2, Ireland (a division of Penguin Books Ltd.)
Penguin Group (Australia), 250 Camberwell Road, Camberwell, Victoria 3124, Australia
(a division of Pearson Australia Group Pty. Ltd.)
Penguin Books India Pvt. Ltd., 11 Community Centre, Panchsheel Park, New Delhi—110 017, India
Penguin Group (NZ), Cnr. Airborne and Rosedale Roads, Albany, Auckland 1310, New Zealand
(a division of Pearson New Zealand Ltd.)
Penguin Books (South Africa) (Pty.) Ltd., 24 Sturdee Avenue, Rosebank, Johannesburg 2196,
South Africa

Penguin Books Ltd., Registered Offices: 80 Strand, London WC2R 0RL, England

HELL ON WHEELS

A Berkley Book / published by arrangement with the author

PRINTING HISTORY
Berkley edition / September 2006

Copyright © 2006 by Peter Brandvold.

ISBN: 0-425-21217-3

BERKLEY®
Berkley Books are published by The Berkley Publishing Group,
a division of Penguin Group (USA) Inc.,
375 Hudson Street, New York, New York 10014.
BERKLEY is a registered trademark of Penguin Group (USA) Inc.
The "B" design is a trademark belonging to Penguin Group (USA) Inc.

PRINTED IN THE UNITED STATES OF AMERICA

10 9 8 7 6 5 4 3 2 1

*For Matt Brandvold,
my cousin and gun expert*

PROLOGUE

BLUE LIGHTNING FLASHED, relieving for an instant the gauzy darkness and lighting the medieval-like stone walls and towers of the territorial prison nestled at the base of black mountains, like the figment of a deranged child's fantasy.

Webster Prewitt, city sheriff of Deer Lodge, Montana Territory, stood on the roofed stoop before his small log office building, a stone mug of black coffee steaming in his leathery fist. He stared south along the town's main drag, at the rain-lashed fortress looming seventy yards away, at the very edge of Deer Lodge proper.

The lightning flashed again, lighting the entire sky and silhouetting the distant mountains. In that instant, Prewitt saw three figures standing before the prison's open front gate, under the arching stone portal. Two wore uniforms and side arms, prison badges flashing on their breasts.

The other was tall, lean, and gray-haired, wearing a long black coat and high-topped boots. He had no hat, and a canvas war bag hung off his shoulder by a rope strap.

Laughter and muffled snippets of conversation drifted to the sheriff's ears between wind gusts. Another lightning flash revealed the man with the bag shaking hands with one of the guards. In the ensuing darkness, another laugh, more boisterous conversation.

Prewitt sipped his coffee and slid his gaze left, to the other side of the street.

A long line of riders waited before the hulking livery barn and scattered corrals. They were mere silhouettes between lightning flares, but when they'd passed before his office twenty minutes ago, Prewitt had counted eleven riders—ten well-armed men on mud-streaked horses, and one girl with long, brown hair under a black felt sombrero and wearing an oilskin rain slicker. Most appeared very young in spite of their unkempt beards, muttonchops, and mustaches. At the head of the pack had ridden a big, burly gent wearing a buffalo coat and a bullet-crowned black hat.

Now the motley gang sat their fidgety mounts, facing the prison. They sat as still as wind- and rain-whipped statues . . . waiting.

Boots thumped the floor behind Prewitt, who turned to see his short, lanky deputy, Kirby Danaher, limp up behind him and lean out the open, lantern-lit doorway, his own coffee mug in his hand. Sucking on the cigarette stuck in the corner of his mouth, Danaher canted his head to see around Prewitt, squinting out through the slanting rain.

"What's happening out there, Boss?"

Prewitt stared southward along the muddy street becoming a stream. Lightning flashed, and he could see the tall, gray-headed man, boots splashing in puddles as he lifted his collar against the rain and walked across the road toward the riders lined up before the barn.

"I don't know," Prewitt said, scowling into the storm. Ruminating on the well-armed riders, he added, "I don't know, Kirby. You tell me. . . ."

•   •   •

Sitting his speckle-gray at the middle of the group, Cole Whateley spit chew into the rain and regarded the tall man moving toward him. His brother, Angus, had turned completely gray during his years behind Deer Lodge's stone walls, his eyes dark chips in his rough-angled face. Improbably, he also seemed straighter, broader, his shoulders more square, his legs and hands thicker. Years of breaking quarry rock had not weakened the man, as Cole had expected. It appeared to have toughened him.

"Everybody here?" Angus asked. He'd stopped before Cole's horse after thunder had boomed on the heels of another lightning flash, and glanced right and left along the line of riders.

"All that could be, Angus," Cole said, rain dripping from his shaggy beard. Because it seemed the proper thing to say to a brother you hadn't seen in five long years, he added, "You look like you came through it all right."

Angus said nothing, just stood regarding the group with his inscrutable eyes, sizing them up, emotionless, though they were all family he hadn't seen in a long, long time.

"How you been, Pap?" said Angus's twenty-year-old son, Quinn, with a tentative air.

Angus's hard eyes found the lad. "How you expect me to be?"

Rain sluicing off his weathered hat, Quinn lowered his sheepish gaze and nodded.

"Pap," Quinn's brother, Wayne, said, touching his hat brim. "Been a long—"

"We'll get re'quainted later," Angus grumbled under the storm, moving to the one riderless horse, the reins of which Cole was holding, and throwing his war bag over the saddle and securing the strap to the horn. Glancing at Cole, he said, "Bring the possibles I wrote ye for?"

"It's all in your saddlebags," Cole said. "Your saber's on the left side of your saddle, wrapped in burlap."

Angus nodded, poked his left boot through the stirrup,

and heaved himself stiffly into the saddle. No doubt, he hadn't ridden a horse for as long as he'd been in prison. Once mounted, he sat there for a moment, shifting his weight, getting reacquainted with the saddle, adjusting his grip on the reins.

"All right," he said finally, casting a wave to the two guards still standing before the prison gate. "Let's ride."

As Angus reined his horse into the street and right, heading north, Cole said, "Ride? Where the hell we ridin' to in this weather?"

"Just ride, brother," Angus said over his shoulder as Cole wheeled his paint into a trot. "I got it all figured out."

"I say we hole up here in town till the storm blows over," Cole yelled above a thunderclap, holding his horse's reins taut as more thunder rumbled over the prison. "With all this lightnin', one of us is liable to get—"

He stopped as his brother turned a savage look to him, long teeth bared, eyes glassy with sudden rage. "I said *ride!*" Angus shouted, and heeled his copper-bay into a lunging gallop between the business district's tall facades.

Cole tensed in his saddle. He stared at his brother galloping off into the rain, then shook his head and yelled to the others, "You heard the man—put the steel to 'em!"

Cole sent his own soggy mount lunging off after Angus's silhouette dwindling in the pouring rain between lamp-lit windows lining the main drag. Horses tethered to the town's three saloons bolted and pulled at their reins, startled by the riders yelling and cursing at their tired, frightened mounts, urging them into loose-gaited lopes. Several of the gang caromed so close to the sheriff's office that mud washed up over the stoop, splattering Sheriff Prewitt and Deputy Danaher with the street's greasy, pungent mix of dung and mud.

"Oh, for the love o' God!" Danaher exclaimed, leaping back and scowling down at his soiled gray trousers. "Of all the low-down crazy stunts!"

Prewitt had jumped back, as well, scowling at the mud on his broadcloth trousers and black boots. He was more interested in the riders than his pants, however, and he scowled after the gang splashing into the distance.

A lightning bolt lashed the sky at that end of town, and thunder clapped like giant trains coupling. One of the fleeing riders' horses whinnied and reared, and the rider rolled off the horse's left hip, hitting the street with an angry yell and a splash. The man who'd been riding to his right whooped and grabbed the riderless horse. He wheeled and returned to the unseated man climbing heavily to his feet and scraping mud from his pants with his gloved hands.

"Where'd you learn to ride, Buck Henry?"

"Goddamned nag!" rose the unseated rider's cry as he caught his tossed reins. "I shoulda known that Billings horse trader was sellin' me a bill of goods!"

He climbed into the leather, and he and his older brother, who gave another excited whoop, put the spurs to their skittish mounts, galloping after the others, who had now disappeared into the wind-buffeted rain and darkness.

"Who in blazes are they?" Prewitt said, rubbing his jaw.

"I don't know, but if I see 'em again, I'm gonna write 'em up for violating city ordinance one-forty—"

"I remember," Prewitt said. He gazed thoughtfully into the rain and darkness as the last hoofbeats faded and another lightning bolt snapped. "Don't know the others, but the man who just got his walkin' papers was some Whateley fella. What was his first name? Angus. Angus Whateley. Warden Brimley told me about him during our weekly poker game. Whateley was part o' that work detail the warden sent over to build our extra cell block last month. Missouri fella. Ran roughshod with his brothers durin' the border wars of the mid-sixties, with the Youngers and Frank James. We talked about him 'cause I remarked how he looked like Wyatt Earp."

"What was the damn fool in for?"

"Stock theft," Prewitt said. "His two boys were hung up on the Hi-Line, for killing two deputies trying to arrest them."

"You don't say," Danaher said. He'd set his coffee down and was wiping the mud from his pants with a newspaper. "Doesn't surprise me. The way they rode outta here, splashin' us like that, ruinin' a good pair of trousers, is good indication they have no respect for no one—includin' the law!"

Ignoring Danaher and still staring into the rain as he sipped his tepid coffee, Prewitt said, "Who's the sheriff on the Hi-Line these days? In Clantick, I mean. Hill County sheriff."

"Last I heard it was Stillman," Danaher said, balling up the soiled newspaper and tossing it into the street, where the wind immediately grabbed it and rolled it up against a white-socked dun tethered before the Good Luck Saloon. "I was gonna wear these trousers over to Mary's folks' place tomorrow night!"

"I think I better wire him," Prewitt said.

"Who's that?"

"Stillman. I think I'd better let him know Whateley's out."

Danaher looked at the sheriff. "You think he's headin' that way?"

Prewitt shook his head. "I don't know where he's headin', but he's headin' somewhere awful fast. I know if he and that woolly crew were headin' my way at that speed, I'd wanna know about it."

With that, Prewitt tossed his coffee dregs into the street and reached into the jailhouse for his rain slicker.

"Hey, wait a sec, Sheriff."

"What is it?"

Danaher wore a thoughtful expression, one boot propped on the chair beside the open door. "I was talkin' with some- body else the other day. He mentioned he heard Stillman and Judge Bannon was over to Sulfur for some high-yapper's weddin'."

Prewitt frowned. "Stillman and *Bannon*?"

Danaher's expression turned grave. "Would Bannon be the judge that hung that Whateley hombre's sons?"

Prewitt turned quickly, stepped off the porch, and strode north through the creeklike street, heading for the Western Union office.

He returned only a few minutes later, his face blanched, eyes scowling. The deputy was sitting back in the sheriff's swivel chair, reading an illustrated newspaper folded open on his lap.

"Back so soon, Sheriff?"

"Damn lines are down," Prewitt said. "This weather." Angrily, he unbuttoned his slicker and stared toward the cell block. "If that gang is headed for Sulfur, Stillman and Bannon have holy hell comin' down around their ears!"

Angus Whateley led the gang, crouched over their saddle horns in the knifing rain, northwest along the main stage road from Deer Lodge. A mile from town, he turned right onto a forking trail that was little more than a two-track wagon trace. It led up into low, wooded hills, climbing higher into heavy pine forests and jagged, granite cliffs.

After an hour's hard ride they descended to a wide, dark valley in which a small ranch headquarters sat. Angus checked his horse down to a walk as he entered the muddy yard in which the lever of a hand pump stood near a stock trough, glistening as though fresh from a smithy's forge in a sudden lightning flash.

The unpainted buildings and corrals huddled in a semi-circle, barraged by the wind and spitting rain. Soft yellow light illuminated the cabin's rain-streaked first-story windows. Angus slowed his horse to a halt as the others rode up behind him, their hooves making sucking sounds in the heavy mud.

He stared at the cabin. The door opened, and a tall, thin figure stepped onto the porch with a lantern. The man stood holding the door open, gazing at the group gathered before him. Finally, he swung the lantern from side to side.

Angus nodded at the silent signal and turned to Cole. "This is the place. We'll bed down in the barn."

"What place?"

"Brother-in-law of one of the prison guards."

"You cozied up to a prison guard?"

"Saved him from taking a sharpened chair leg in the back. We fought in the same company durin' the War."

Angus dismounted from the wet horse, lifted the barn's latching bar, opened the doors, and waved the others inside. A lantern hung on a square-hewn joist, turned low. Angus turned up the flame, lighted a second lantern, and in a few minutes the horses were stalled with fresh hay, oats, and water.

The men and the lone girl wasted no time rolling out their blankets, which they'd kept moderately dry with heavy burlap. Angus stood near the open door, smoking a cigarette he'd rolled from Cole's makings.

"We ride at first light. I take it you're all good with shootin' irons. No Whateley ever not been handy with a firearm."

The others, shivering as they stripped out of their wet shirts and denims, nodded. Angus glanced at the girl, Temple Brindle, then shifted his gaze to Temple's father, Angus's gray-bearded brother-in-law. T.L. Brindle peeled off his shabby blanket coat and draped it over a stall partition. He was clad in baggy homespuns and wore an old Colt Patterson on his hip. He'd fought nearly to the death at Stone's River and Shiloh, and a Yankee saber had cut a straight line down the far left side of his face.

"T.L., can that girl work a lead pusher?"

"She can shoot the eyeball out of a runnin' jackrabbit at

a hundred yards," Brindle said, puffing a corncob pipe. "That's why I brung her along."

"Hell, T.L., you brung her along to keep her from gettin' in the family way again!" jeered Cole's towheaded son, Buck Henry. He was sixteen and barely five-foot-five, but he was hard as a whipstock, with glinting gray flint for eyes.

"That's enough o' that talk, damn your scrawny hide!" Brindle shouted, pointing a threatening finger at the boy.

The other sons of Angus and Cole laughed, glancing at the mute girl, who appeared to have heard none of it as she undressed behind a stall partition, her unkempt hair waving about her shoulders.

"Enough foolishness!" Angus shouted. "You're all too young to have fought in the Great War for Southern Independence. You're soft and you're weak. But you're soldiers now, to a man. Tomorrow we go after the judge who ordered the unjustified hangin's of your innocent cousins and brothers. Get to sleep. Rain or shine, we ride at first cock crow!"

When Angus had hunkered down to go through his saddlebags, Cole knelt down beside him. "Where is this judge, Angus?"

"Little town of Sulfur. Thirty, forty-mile ride from here, northwest." Angus pulled an old .44 Remington revolver and his war-torn campaign hat from his saddlebag. He shaped the threadbare kepi and tried it on. "The guard told me he was down there for some weddin' or funeral or some such. Nice piece of luck. If he was at home in Chinook, we'd have us another two, three-day ride. As it is, I figure to ambush his stage on his way home."

"Who else we goin' after?"

"That's it," Angus said. He'd removed his hat and was sliding his Confederate-gray trousers from the saddlebag. He chuffed with disgust. "I'd sure love to kill Hobbs, the rancher in cahoots with Bannon. But the lawman with the judge—Stillman—already done it some years ago." His eyes turned dark. "Just Bannon. Stillman, too, if he gets in the way . . ."

Later, after the lights had been extinguished and several snores sounded in the musty darkness, Angus's oldest son, Wayne, nudged his cousin, Vernon, lying beside him. "That's what I figured Pap called us out here for. We're goin' after the law that hung Earl and Thaddeus."

"Hell, that's so long ago now, I hardly remember Earl and Thaddeus."

"Gotta admit, my memory's a little dim. But they were family. Their killin' got be set right."

"I ain't arguin' with you there, Cuz," Vernon said. He sat against a post, twirling his old .36 Spiller and Burr percussion revolver on his finger—an old Confederate war pistol he'd found in the tack room back at the farm and with which he'd become a fair shot. It was Vernon's dream to become a hired gun and hide in the Indian Nations between assignments and victims. It beat rustling cattle and following a mule and a plow around a cornfield. "This is just the kind of action I been waitin' for." He chuckled softly. "Hell, drillin' daylight through a judge is the best reputation a regulator could ask for!"

There was a long pause. The rain rattled the barn roof. Cole and T.L. Brindle snored nearly as loud as the fading thunder.

"Don't get me wrong, Vernon," Wayne said after a while. "But Pa—he looks crazier than a tree full of owls."

Vernon glanced through the half-open barn doors. Uncle Angus stood outside, just before the doors, his head and arms thrown back as he let the rain sluicing off the roof wash over his face. He stood tall, his wet hair blown wild, and his craggy but vigorous countenance glowed ghostly in the intermittent lightning flashes.

"I'm comin', Judge," he said just loudly enough for Wayne and Vernon to hear him above the storm. "I'm comin' . . . jest like I promised!"

1

BELLIED UP TO the bar in the Continental Saloon in Sulfur, Montana, Ben Stillman sipped his beer and ran a hand through his collar-length, salt-and-pepper hair, then smoothed his brushy mustache.

He was about to answer a smart remark made by Dr. Clyde Evans, standing to Stillman's right and chasing a beer with single-cut rye, when something caught Stillman's eye out the saloon's broad front windows.

"What is it, Ben?" Evans asked.

Stillman didn't say anything. He directed his keen, blue-eyed gaze at the batwings, through which three men dressed in dusty trail garb entered the saloon's early morning quiet.

The Continental's working girls were still asleep up-stairs after a boisterous Saturday night. A few miners in billed hats and hobnailed boots played a leisurely poker game in the shadows against the wall to Stillman's right. The barkeep, a tall, walleyed gent named Johnson, plopped pickled eggs into the three-gallon jar across the bar from Evans.

Stillman sized up the three men sauntering toward him through the tables upon which the chairs were still stacked. A massive hombre wearing a Mexican poncho and a funnel-brimmed hat. A stringbean with gray eyes bulging from their sockets, and shotgun chaps. A short man, barely over five feet, with a nose the size of a hickory knot and a droopy, sand-colored mustache.

The three wore pistols thonged low on their hips. Wide-bladed knives jutted from worn leather sheaths. Their spurs chinged against the saloon's scuffed puncheons.

Slowly tucking his frock coat back behind his long-barreled .44 positioned for the cross-draw on his left hip, Stillman glanced at Evans. "Doc, edge back down the bar there, will you?"

Evans stared at the three approaching hardcases, the doctor's eyes pensive behind his gold-framed spectacles. He took a slow step back, stopped, and reached for his beer and shot glass. He slid the drinks down the bar as he backed slowly away from Stillman, his gaze glued to the three men halting six feet away from the bar and brushing their dusters back from their revolvers.

The three regarded Stillman with barely contained belligerence. One elbow propped casually atop the mahogany, Stillman met their gazes without expression.

The short man said, "You're Ben Stillman, ain't ye?" His voice was deep, gruff, and hollow. He had a face the texture of an old hide sofa, one cheek bulging with chew.

The dead-snake and stale-alcohol stench of the three men burned Stillman's nose. "Who's asking?"

The short man glanced at the other two, returned his gaze to Stillman. "Friends of Boone Early."

After a few seconds, Stillman nodded slowly. The names and faces of the men he'd taken down through the long years he'd spent behind a deputy U.S. marshal's badge were seared into his brain like a brand in a steer's hide.

"Let's see," he said, thoughtfully rubbing his jaw.

"Boone . . . he was pret' near ten years ago now. As I recall, he was wanted for raping a widow's daughter from Belle Fourche. Drew down on me in a roadhouse near Elk Ridge."

"Hellkatoot," the big man grunted. "Boone didn't need to *take* his women. One glance at his handsome mug, they went willinglike."

Stillman said nothing. He'd been through it all before countless times—friends and family of those he'd either killed or sent to the state pen in Deer Lodge seeking restitution for those who didn't deserve it. The ex-marshal and current sheriff of Hill County, in the Montana Territory, had never killed anyone who hadn't thrown down on him first or hadn't been about to kill someone else.

And he'd never knowingly arrested anyone who hadn't deserved jail time or the hangman's noose.

No point in trying to convince these three, though. They'd made up their minds a long time ago to avenge Early, and the stagger juice they'd been drinking all night had fueled their fires.

Stillman thought briefly of his wife, Fay, and what would happen to her if he finally lost the war today—her being in the family way now, too. She was waiting for him over at the Palace Hotel, her bags packed and ready to hop the stage back to Clantick.

The big man—a good three or four inches over Stillman's six-one—sniffed and snarled, "Ain't seen you around in a long time, Marshal. Been hidin' out?" He grinned.

The short man repositioned the quid in his cheek and said dully, "Why, I heard he done caught a bullet in his back six, seven years ago. Almost died, nearly crippled. Had to hang up his guns for a while; then he got him a job sheriffin' up north. Hill County, ain't it?"

He smiled, his small, cracked teeth brown as runny dog turds. "Married him a purty French girl. Long, black hair, jugs out to here."

The stringbean snickered. The big man guffawed.

"She's gonna be lonely once you're gone, *Sheriff*," the stringbean said through a snort, elbowing the brute. "Maybe me and Elwin and Dewey better stick around town, *comfort* her after you been turned down with the snakes, if 'n you get my drift."

He winked and grinned.

Glancing at Stillman's implacable visage, Evans whistled softly and moved back toward the other end of the bar.

Stillman expelled a breath. He hated killing, but there was no way around these three.

He scowled and said, "If you boys are lookin' to snuggle with the snakes, get to it, will you? I find your conversation downright dull, and phew—do you boys stink!"

The three flushed deep crimson. The short man's mustache contracted as his jaws tightened.

Evans muttered, "Oh, boy," and retreated even farther, sliding his beer and whiskey along the bar.

In spite of the fire kindled just behind his heart, Stillman maintained a neutral expression, and waited. Moving stiffly and slowly, arms hanging straight down at their sides, the three men took two steps back and put at least two feet between them. The big man hipped a table out of his way, the wooden legs barking across the puncheons. A chair toppled with a crash. Eyes fixed on Stillman, the big man ignored it.

Out of the corner of his right eye, Stillman saw the miners scurry away from their table, muttering in a foreign tongue and dropping back into the shadows a safe distance away from the imminent gunfire. Out of the corner of his left eye, Stillman saw the barkeep, Johnson, hustle down the bar until he stood across from Evans.

Evans threw back the last of his rye and set the shot glass gently back on the bar. Holding his breath, he stared at the tense scene before him.

Each of the three hardcases stood about ten feet from Stillman, forming a near half circle around him. The lawman stood with his back to the bar, feet spread a little

wider than his shoulders, frock coat pushed back behind
the walnut-gripped Colt riding high, butt forward, on his
left hip.

His high-crowned, broad-brimmed Stetson was tipped
slightly back, giving him a good view from beneath the
brim. His weathered, handsome face was impassive as
granite. The only movement was the subtle dimpling of his
left jaw hinge.

Evans couldn't see Stillman's eyes, but he knew they
were roving not over the gunmen's hands but across their
faces. Stillman had told the doctor that he could always tell
when a man was going to draw on him by a faint light flick-
ering behind the eyes.

Hands twitched involuntarily, but the eyes gave away
the conscious intention.

Apparently, the big man drew first. Evans saw the heavy
arm twitch, the revolver just beginning to clear leather before Stillman, effecting a border draw with no wasted ges-
tures, reached across his belly with his right hand and
clawed the Colt from the holster on his left hip. The .44
Colt came up so fast it was only a blur before it popped and
smoked.

The big man lunged back with a grunt, dropping his
own weapon and clutching his chest, heavy boots pounding, spurs raucously chinging on the floor. As he went
down, Stillman turned sharply right and shot the stringbean, whose short-barreled, silver-plated revolver hadn't
climbed any higher than the big man's.

The stringbean gave a wail as he twisted sideways and
flung his revolver high and behind him. It bounced off
a chair as the thin man bounded four steps toward the
batwings and dropped to his knees, clutching his belly and
yelling, "Oh! Mercy, no!"

Stillman pivoted left, extending the Colt at the short man.
The short man brought his long-barreled Remington up.

"Uh-uh," Stillman grunted, aiming his Colt at the short

man's forehead. The man froze, the gun only belly high, the single-action revolver's hammer not yet cocked. Apparently, Stillman had seen the fearful hesitation in the man's eyes and was going to give him a chance to surrender.

The short man stared at Stillman. Then his mustache drew back from his lips, and the fear in his eyes was replaced by rage. As he jerked his gun up, Stillman shot him through his right shoulder.

The short man grunted, staggered back, and dropped to his right knee, his pistol still in his hand. Raking air in and out of his lungs, he glared up at Stillman. "Ye bastard son of a bitch!"

Stillman extended his Colt at the short man's head. "Raise that gun, and you're wolf bait."

The short man's eyes grew thoughtful. "All right, all right," he said. He began lowering the pistol, then raised it again quickly.

Before he had the weapon fully extended, Stillman pulled his Colt's trigger. The slug plowed through the man's forehead and exited the rear of the skull in a blood-and-brain spray that painted the floor a half second before the short man fell on top of it. He flopped like a landed fish and quivered.

The stringbean, sobbing, knelt before the batwings. He studied his bloody middle and sobbed and wailed, "Ma! The bastard shot me through the guts . . . I'm coming to join ye!"

Evans found himself crouching beside the bar, one hand on the bar top, staring with mute fascination and horror at the gun smoke webbing over the dead and dying. Time had slowed to a near standstill, and he guessed that less than ten seconds had passed since the big man had clawed iron. His heart thudding, the doctor straightened, grabbed his beer off the bar, and downed it in a single pull.

Stillman lowered his revolver, gave the two dead men a cursory inspection, and walked over to the stringbean bent forward on his knees, arms crossed on his stomach, crying into the sawdust-sprinkled floor.

Stillman bent down, removed the knife from the man's belt sheath, and skidded the big bowie across the floor. Footsteps sounded to his left and he looked up to see Evans approach, staring down at the wounded man. The medico's broad, mustachioed face was flushed from nerves and drink.

"How bad?" Evans inquired. For all his drinking, gambling, and womanizing, he was first and foremost a doctor.

"Gut-shot," Stillman grouched. "I overcompensated for the first shot's recoil. He's dyin' ugly."

Evans knelt on the other side of the stringbean, grabbed the man's collar, and gently pulled back, lifting the man's head off the floor.

"Oh, Christ, it hurts!" the wounded man bellowed.

Boots pounded the boardwalk outside the saloon. Stillman turned to the batwings as a short, gray-haired gent in a crisp bowler and fawn vest trimmed with a tin sheriff's star and a gold watch chain pushed through the gawkers gathered before the doors. Dan Price, Sulfur County sheriff, hurried into the saloon wielding a double-barreled shotgun, a peeved scowl drawing the corners of his mouth down.

He elbowed a path through the miners, who'd stepped out from the wall to inspect Stillman's handiwork, exclaiming amongst themselves. He peered into the smoky shadows and muttered, "What in the hell—?"

The sheriff stopped when his eyes found Stillman kneeling beside the stringbean. "Ben . . . ?"

"Old friends of mine," Stillman dryly quipped, glancing at the two dead men sprawled nearby.

Understanding flickered in Price's eyes. He lowered his barn blaster and grunted, "Shit. In my town? Sorry, Ben."

"Sorry about the mess," Stillman said, straightening and holstering his Colt.

When Price had sent one of the miners for the Sulfur

sawbones and the undertaker, he returned his gaze to Stillman, shook his head, and tugged at a corner of his carefully trimmed, silver-gray mustache. "We're either huntin'
or gettin' hunted. Jumpin' Jehosaphat—why do we stay in
this racket?"

Stillman chuffed without mirth as he watched the gut-
shot stringbean writhing in pain. "What else we gonna do,
Dan—sell stationery?"

Price dropped his gaze to the sobbing stringbean, who,
between Stillman-directed epithets, kept calling out to his
mother. "Took a pill he couldn't digest, eh? He gonna make
it, Doc?"

Evans stood and shook his head. "He's joining his ma."

"Good." Price looked at Stillman. "You boys' stage is
fixin' to pull out. Why don't you hightail? Me an' my
deputies'll take care of these sorry sons o' bitches."

"I hate to leave you with the mop-up, Dan."

"Hell, I don't have nothin' else to do. By the time the
hole's dug for those two, this pathetic bastard'll be ready to
join 'em."

A minute later, Stillman and Evans pushed through the
batwings onto the boardwalk, where only a few gawkers
remained. The Hill County sheriff and the stocky medico
turned east up Sulfur Springs' main drag, lengthening their
strides for the stage depot.

"No word to the women, eh, Doc?"

"Mum's the word."

As he hurried to match Stillman's pace, Evans brushed
at the sawdust on the knees of his shabby dress slacks.
"I've said it before, I'll say it again—I don't see how you
walk around every day with a target on your back. Hell,
just watching what you did in there nearly killed me dead-
er'n a beaver hat."

"You get used to it," Stillman lied, thinking again about
Fay. She was no doubt waiting for him aboard the stage—
her and their other two traveling companions, the doctor's

sometime lady friend, Katherine Kemmett, and Crystal Harmon.

Stillman stepped off the boardwalk and paused to let an ore wagon pass. "I'll tell you one thing, though."

"What's that?"

"I'm ready for a nice, quiet ride in the country."

Walking abreast, they angled across the rutted street toward the waiting stagecoach parked before the depot, the stout Concord flaunting its red, gold, and yellow colors in the bright morning sun.

"Far from the madding crowd," Evans said. Producing a leather flask from his back pocket, he popped the cork and took a long pull, his Adam's apple bobbing slowly. Lowering the flask, he smacked his lips and sucked the whiskey from his thick, red mustache. "Me, too."

2

INSIDE THE STAGECOACH that rocked and rattled north through the chalky buttes and sage-tufted benches of central Montana, Evans fumbled around in his vest pocket for his whiskey flask. Finding it, he popped the cork and extended the hide-wrapped canteen to Stillman, sitting across from him.

"Nip?"

The doctor's cinnamon brows arched expectantly behind his spectacles, which had acquired another sheen of dust since he'd last cleaned them with his fingers. Stillman regarded Evans dully. After what he'd just been through, he was in no mood for the doctor's shenanigans.

Evans knew, as everybody did, that Stillman had given up hard booze years ago. The doctor was only giving Katherine Kemmett—who rode stiffly beside him with her hands in her lap—a dig.

Stillman didn't say anything. He wished like hell Evans would mind his p's and q's until the stage pulled into Clantick. As a matter of fact, it was Evans's behavior he'd intended to discuss with the doctor over drinks in the Continental, before he'd been so rudely interrupted.

Between Clyde's drinking and Stillman getting ambushed by a bunch of drunken hardcases, it had been a long weekend. He glanced at Fay's refreshingly placid face, glad that she knew nothing of what had happened.

Stillman and Fay had ridden with Evans, Katherine, Crystal Harmon, and Mr. and Mrs. Judge John Bannon a hundred miles south to Sulfur, across the Missouri River, to attend the wedding of Dick Madsen, a former Clantick businessman and friend. Crystal had stayed with her aunt, while Stillman and Fay, the judge and Mrs. Bannon, and the doctor and Katherine had stayed at the Missouri Hotel.

It was at the hotel, the night after Madsen's wedding, that the trouble between Clyde and Katherine had started. It didn't look like it was going to end any time soon. Now Katherine gave Evans exactly what he'd baited her for—a disapproving scowl.

"Oh, Clyde!" she exclaimed. "Haven't you had *enough*?"

"What do you mean by 'enough,' Katherine?" Evans asked her mockingly, his glasses glinting dustily in the light angling over a morning-purple rimrock beyond the window. "Define 'enough.' "

She chuffed with disgust and looked away. The widow of a Lutheran pastor, Katherine Kemmett was in her mid-thirties, several years younger than Evans, though her rigid, prudish countenance made her seem older. She worked as a midwife and as Evans's nurse, and there seemed to be something romantic between them, but Stillman wasn't sure what that something was. As far as he could tell, they got along about as well as dynamite and lightning.

She glowered at him now, the corners of her mouth drawn down, making her look fifty.

Inwardly, Stillman clenched. The widow's open disapproval only egged the medico on. Stillman knew what was coming, and come it did as the doctor took the flask between thumb and index finger of his right hand. He lifted it to his mouth, capped by a sweeping, red mustache, and tipped it back with a flourish.

He swallowed once, hard, lowered the flask with a satisfied sigh, and corked it. Smacking his lips, he returned the flask to his vest.

"Oh!" Katherine exclaimed. Her plain features blanched as she rolled her eyes with disgust and snapped her head to the window so hard that she nearly lost her small, feathered hat.

"I think how Katherine would define 'enough,' Doctor," Fay Stillman said, sitting beside her husband, a gloved hand hooked through his arm, "is enough whiskey in three days to float a clipper ship and to raise the oceans a conservative inch."

A faint smile accompanied the observation, lighting up Fay's classically beautiful face with its full lips, almond eyes, and frame of rich, chocolate hair. She was nine weeks pregnant, and an inner aura made her French-dark beauty appear even more exotic and alluring.

Her lustrous brown eyes narrowed. She regarded the doctor with ironic derision. "Enough to make the proprietor of the hotel saloon much happier today than he was last Friday, at least."

Evans's face colored, and small lines formed above his nose. Stillman chuckled, as did Judge Bannon, sitting across from him. Bannon was a middle-aged man of average height whose penchant for nightly sirloins, port whiskey, and Cuban cigars had given him the florid, portly countenance of a retired sea captain. The judge played weekly poker with Evans and was familiar with the doctor's foibles.

"Sorry, Doc," Stillman said. "I'll try to get my wife under control at the first stage stop."

Fay nudged him with her elbow.

Crystal Harmon, the pretty, tomboyish blonde who ranched with her husband, Jody, south of Clantick, chuckled openly. She was sitting on the other side of Fay, next to the door and directly across from Katherine Kemmett. "If I remember right, you promised to behave yourself this weekend, Doc."

Still a little a goosey from the shooting in the Continental, and made even more uncomfortable by the derision aimed at him, the doctor squirmed in his seat, cleared his throat, and curled a lip at the girl. "Define 'behave.'"

"Uh-oh. What did you do, Doc?" Crystal asked huskily. "From Aunt Lenore's place, I didn't hear any fire bells. . . ."

"He didn't set the town on fire," Katherine said, her features set with scolding. "But he did just about everything else, the details of which are best forgotten." She condemned Evans with another look. "Dis*gusting* man!"

Evans smiled sheepishly at Crystal. "I lost a few bucks at the faro tables after the wedding dance."

Katherine snapped her head at him. "A *few*?"

Evans frowned, shrugged, dropped his gaze with chagrin. "A few of mine, a few of .· . . Katherine's."

"A hundred dollars of his own money, and twenty of mine," Katherine explained. "And then he got tighter than I've ever seen him . . . even *him* . . . and he—" Katherine stopped herself, shook her head, and turned to the window. "No, it's too disgusting to talk about in civilized company."

"Yes," Judge Bannon said, lowering his double chin and regarding Evans from under his shaggy brows. "I think it's best if we all forget about the night Clantick's sole medical professional nearly got himself thrown out of the Missouri Hotel in Sulfur."

"Oh, please!" Katherine said, covering her ears and shaking her head.

"Must we talk about it, John?" Bannon's wife said, pouting, turning to him with her plucked, arched brows.

Mrs. Bannon was the former Prudence Desmond, a dance-hall girl the judge had met last year in Virginia City, the year after his wife had died of blood poisoning. Young enough to be Bannon's daughter, she was a pale, full-figured brunette decked out in a powder-blue traveling smock with a matching feathered hat and Turkish walking boots.

After the wedding, the former dance-hall girl with a storied past had wasted little time in acquiring airs and a difficult, standoffish disposition for which she was infamous around Clantick. Few townswomen liked her, but they tried to get along as the judge was a generally admired and respected member of the community.

"Sorry, my dear . . . Mrs. Kemmett," Bannon said, sheepish.

Never one to conceal her feelings, Crystal hung her jaw, her blue eyes flashing with surprise. "Thrown *out*?"

Evans glanced at Stillman as if for help. The sheriff only shrugged. Evans scowled and twiddled his thumbs in his lap. "I wouldn't say I was exactly thrown out," he muttered. "It was more like . . . escorted . . ."

"To the door," Fay finished for him, holding her darkly ironic gaze on him steadily as the stage jostled them all from side to side. "At three in the morning."

"Oh!" Katherine exclaimed, throwing up her hands again as she stared out the window.

"Doctor, good heavens," Mrs. Bannon said, as though the medico had just broken wind.

Crystal toyed with the tightly wound bun at the back of her neck. She usually wore her straw-colored hair straight down her back and under a man's felt Stetson. Also more accustomed to riding a saddle than a carriage, she enjoyed this diversion in what would be an otherwise boring ride.

"What on earth did you do to get yourself thrown out of the hotel at three in the morning, Doc?" she asked, for Katherine's sake trying not to smile.

Stillman had been trying hard to contain his mirth, but somehow a low chuckle snuck out of his throat. Fay, Katherine, and Mrs. Bannon snapped their heads at him, brows sternly knit.

Stillman slid his gaze to each, lifted his hands from his knees, and shrugged innocently. He tried to wipe his mind clear of the image of the doctor pounding on Katherine's hotel room door early Sunday morning, demanding she let him in, shouting, *"You know you want a tumble as much as I do, lady!"* A suppressed chuckle wracked the sheriff. He was dangerously close to losing his composure and probably his place in his own bed for the next few nights.

Stillman glanced at Bannon, who offered a half wink. The Hill County sheriff choked back another involuntary chuckle at the memory, scratched his cheek, and turned to the window on his side of the stage.

Evans turned to Stillman angrily. "Ben, you're a legendary lawman. You've taken down more badmen than Wyatt Earp, but here you are, abandoning me to these . . . *she-wolves!* Are you going to let these women cow you into turning your back on a friend?" He turned to Bannon. "You, too, Judge?"

Stillman glanced from the doctor to Fay to Katherine. Both women's brows were arched with looks of reproof and expectation, as though waiting for him to choose sides. He looked from one to the other once more, glanced at young Crystal, who eagerly awaited his response, then turned to the doctor and gave a resolute nod and a tight smile.

"You're on your own, Clyde."

The judge glanced at his wife, then at Evans. Lips pursed with chagrin, he nodded reluctantly and grunted, "Sorry, Doctor."

Grumbling, Evans dug a half-smoked cheroot from the pocket of his corduroy jacket, lit it, and shuttled his gaze to the passing buck brush and sandy buttes. A prairie-dog town appeared, the residents scurrying for their holes as the stage approached. Trying to ignore the women's ceaseless berating, the doctor envied the prairie dogs.

Stillman stared out the same window as Evans, but he didn't see the prairie dogs. Since he'd learned of Fay's pregnancy four months ago, he often found himself fretting about the future, wondering if he'd live to see their child grown.

He'd done a pretty thorough job of taking the teeth out of the little town of Clantick along the banks of the Milk River, and of taming all of Hill County, as well. Still, with all the drifters and owlhoots passing through, it was often a woolly place, so far off the beaten path, and maintaining law and order in such a region was a dangerous task.

Hell, trouble had followed him to Sulfur, when he wasn't even wearing his badge.

When he'd learned that he was going to be a father, Stillman had been overjoyed. Lately, however, he couldn't help seeing, in his mind's eye, visions of Fay dressed in widow's weeds and leading a young child—sometimes a girl in a simple dress and pigtails, sometimes a boy in wool knickers and bullet-crowned hat—up the path to the cemetery where Stillman's bullet-riddled corpse was being laid to rest under the box elders.

The image tied a knot in his gut. He could not, would not leave Fay a widow, their child fatherless. With a family on the way, it was probably time to consider switching professions to something less dangerous.

To what?

He'd been a lawman over half his life. He'd been a soldier for a few years during the War, and he'd driven a few cows and shot a few buffalo, but he'd been a deputy U.S. marshal for nearly twenty years before taking a bullet in the back. The injury had forced his retirement from federal service, but a short time later, after marrying Fay, he'd pinned the sheriff's star to his shirt. All he really knew was law enforcement.

In his mid-forties, he couldn't see himself mucking out livery stalls or swamping saloons. He raised chickens in the converted buggy shed behind his house in Clantick, but he doubted selling eggs and fryers would bring in enough money to support Fay and his child the way he wanted. Fay taught school, but the town couldn't afford to pay her more than fifteen to twenty dollars a month.

Stillman had saved a little money over the years. Maybe he'd buy a small farm or a ranch, a little ten-cow operation nestled in a valley somewhere back in the Two Bears. Near Long John Butte, say—he'd always liked that country. With plenty of timothy and rolling aspen hills. With a coop for his barred rock hens.

And with a little creek running through, so that he, Fay, and their child could stroll along the darkening water at night before bedtime . . .

Stillman's reverie was interrupted by a flash along the lip of a sandstone ridge east of the stage road. He studied the ridge, frowning, his lawman's keen sense of danger prodding him. The flash was probably only the sun reflected off mica or a bottle some cowboy had discarded, but he hadn't remained on the north side of the sod by being careless.

The stage had just bounced and shuddered over a pothole when the piercing pinprick of brassy light shone again, in a slight cleft in the ridge's lip, just up from a talus slide. Stillman stared at it, squinting hard against the glare, until it disappeared a few seconds later.

He blinked the red spots from his retinas. That was no rock reflection. It was more akin to a sun flash off field glasses.

"What is it, Ben?" the judge asked.

Holding his head out the window as he stared at the ridge, Stillman said, "Nothing." No use getting anyone riled.

He pulled his head back in the carriage. Fay glanced at him with a curious frown. He shrugged, patted her hand hooked through his left arm, and settled back in his seat. For the benefit of the other passengers, he manufactured a casual air while keeping one eye peeled on the passing terrain.

The dun ridges along both sides of the road were lowering and drawing away when, several minutes later, Stillman spied movement along a grassy knoll a quarter mile northeast. His heart picking up its pace, he straightened in his seat and squinted out the window, through the dust broiling up from the six-horse hitch and the iron-tired wheels.

A horseback rider galloped over the knoll's crest and disappeared down the other side.

He was riding hard and whipping glances over his shoulder, like a thieving fox with its jaws full of chicken.

3

CASTING ANOTHER GLANCE at the knoll over which the fleeing rider had disappeared, Stillman doffed his hat and stuck his head out the window.

"Fred!" he yelled up to the driver's box. "Check 'em down!"

After a second's hesitation, the jehu called to his team. "Whoa, Skip! Whoa, King! All you hammer-headed son' o' bitches—*whoooo-ahhhhhhhhh!*"

As the coach began slowing, the carriage rocking on its thoroughbraces, the passengers reached for the leather grabs hanging from the ceiling.

Fay placed a hand on Stillman's thigh and arched her dark eyebrows. "What is it?"

"What's going on, Ben?" Judge Bannon inquired, a peevish flush rising from beneath his face's natural mottled rose.

"Probably nothing," Stillman said, leaning forward in his seat, waiting for the coach to stop. "I saw a rider on a hill yonder, and I just want to make sure we're not being set up for a hit."

Prudence Bannon gasped. Her jaw dropped as her face turned as red as her husband's. "A *hit*?"

Stillman winced, immediately wishing he'd been a little more delicate. "I just want to consult with the driver about it, ma'am. No reason to get worked up."

She slapped a hand to her chest, and turned to her husband. "How can I not get worked up about . . . about a *hit*?"

Stillman glanced beseechingly at Fay, who rolled her eyes. As his wife consoled Mrs. Bannon with her velvety voice, the sheriff donned his hat, shoved the door open, and stepped out.

Tipsy from the jolting ride, he closed the door to protect the passengers from as much dust as possible. As he stepped to the front wheel and cast his gaze up to the driver's box, the dust-caked, sunburned driver and shotgun messenger stared down at him. They'd lowered their neckerchiefs, but their expressions were hard to decipher in the shade of their broad hat brims.

"We seen him, Ben," said the driver, Fred Miller. The split ribbons were in his gloved hands, forearms resting on his skinny knees. He was an older gent, so whipcord-thin that his clothes appeared perpetually about to fall from his frame. A large, blood-red birthmark nearly covered his right cheek, the wrinkled skin drawn taut across the bone.

"Probably just a waddy," said the younger shotgun rider, Gilbert Hicks, his double-barreled Greener held in the crook of his left arm. "There's a ranch—the Circle Six— about five miles east."

"He was ridin' like a bat out of hell."

Hicks spit a stream of chew. "Maybe he's late for lunch."

"No reason to hit us," Miller said. "We ain't carryin' nothin' but a mail pouch—aside from you passengers, that is."

Stillman scowled and directed his gaze eastward, where the sage-covered hills rolled up to higher rimrocks along the horizon.

No sign of anyone. No sun flashes.

Up trail, the hills grew higher, rockier, more forested, and were scored with deep clefts.

"The best place to hit us would be where the trail narrows along Elk Creek, wouldn't it?" Stillman said to Miller.

The grizzled driver shrugged. "I reckon." Miller screwed his face up. "But why in the hell would they hit us?"

"Humor me, Fred. A half mile before the trail narrows down, pull off the road. I want to check it out before you run the stage through."

"All right, Ben, but it's a waste o' time if you ask me."

"That'll make us late pullin' into the Rock Creek Station," Hicks complained.

"And late for lunch." Stillman glanced at the young shotgun rider's bulging paunch. "You'll live, Gil."

The sheriff opened the door and climbed back into the stage. A few minutes later, Miller had his team again galloping northward, slowing for the upgrades and sharp turns. Elk Creek curved toward the trail and ran alongside the stage and through aspens before angling off to the right.

As Stillman rode, he wondered about the galloping rider he'd watched disappear over the knoll. As Miller had pointed out, the stage was carrying nothing but human cargo, so robbers could hope to get little more than some ladies' jewelry and pocket jingle.

But like the men Stillman had taken down in the Continental, they could be after him, Stillman himself. A man who rode careless didn't ride long, and neither did those who rode with him.

At the opening of the pass between two high mesas split by the twinkling waters of Elk Creek, bubbling over rocks and beaver dams only a few feet from the trail, Miller

slowed the stage. He pulled left of the trail and stopped in a
sun-dappled aspen grove alive with chittering squirrels and
mountain chickadees.

When Stillman had retrieved his Henry rifle from the
luggage boot, he and Fred Miller legged it up a northern
slope, leaving the other men with the women.

A few minutes later they squatted behind boulders
above the trail hugging the creek a hundred feet below.

"I'll be damned," Miller wheezed under his breath, wiping his sweating brow with the back of his right wrist. He
held a Model '63 seven-shot Spencer carbine in his other
hand. "You were right!"

"This is one time I wish I wasn't so damn smart," Stillman grumbled as he stared downslope.

Directly below, several gunmen squatted and lay prone
along the rocky ledges and shrubs hugging both sides of
the creek and trail. He counted six figures, but hunkered
down as they were for an ambush, it was hard to tell how
many men there were exactly.

The ones Stillman could make out were wielding rifles.
One man—a tall, lean hombre in gray Confederate-style
cavalry slacks and hunkered on his haunches behind several stunt pines and a wagon-sized boulder—wore an ar-
tillery saber in a brass-mounted sheath.

In a wide cut on the other side of the creek, perpendicu-
lar to the trail, a herd of horses was tethered at the edge of
an aspen stand running along a hill flank—at least ten
mounts, maybe a dozen.

Staring and aiming their rifles down trail, they were
awaiting the stage, all right. They were either after a fabled
strongbox or Stillman himself. He recognized none of the
men from this distance, but any or all could have been
hardcases Stillman had sent to Deer Lodge. He doubted
they were after what few valuables the passengers might
have on their persons.

Not a gang this size.

"Time to bust up the party," Stillman said. "Fred, start flinging lead when I give the signal."

Miller nodded as Stillman, crouching, dropped several feet down the ledge and slid back behind a boulder. He secured one brown boot in the gravel and thin soil, planted the other on a low, flat rock, and propped his Henry in a notch in the boulder's brow, aiming downslope.

He couldn't take them all down, and they certainly weren't going to surrender to him. But if they saw he had them out-positioned, he might be able to scatter them, make them think twice about their intentions.

"You in the canyon!" he called. "What in hell's goin' on down there?"

Almost as one, the gang swung toward him. Hatted heads appeared from behind shrubs and boulders. Several surprised grunts and curses rose to Stillman's ears.

"Stay out of it, lawman!" someone yelled, a deep, throaty base cracking with volume.

One man jerked out from the cleft between two rocks so quickly he slipped and fell back. Steadying himself, he snapped his rifle to his shoulder, and aimed at Stillman.

His Winchester puffed smoke. The report reached Stillman the same time the slug barked off a rock a foot to Stillman's right.

"Give 'em hell, Fred," Stillman raked out, tossing away his hat, brushing a lock of hair from his eyes, and lowering a weathered cheek to his Henry's stock inlaid with a pearl bull's head.

As another slug slammed into the rock before him, Stillman triggered the Henry at a burly, bearded man raising a rifle on this side of the creek. The slug buzzed past the man's right ear and thumped into the pine behind him as the man tripped the trigger of his own rifle.

The ambusher's bullet sailed wide as he stumbled back with a start, glancing at the gobbet Stillman had blown from the tree and exclaiming, "Shee-it!"

"Bastards have the high ground!" yelled another man, leaping a boulder and heading for the cut where the horses were tied.

Stillman fired again, and one of the hardcases grabbed his left calf as he fell, then turned and crawled through a crack in the rocks.

"Hold your positions, goddammit!"

As Stillman triggered a shot and levered another shell into the Henry's breech, the tall man with the saber and butternut-gray slacks stood tall before the boulders he'd been crouched against a moment before. He held a big Sharps in both hands, a leather lanyard draped around his neck. He fired. The heavy slug plowed with a screeching pop into a rock six inches left of Fred Miller's face.

The jehu popped off a shot of his own and jerked his head back, squinting against the spraying rock shards and muttering a curse.

"I said hold your damn positions!" the tall man with the buffalo gun roared at his brethren, leaping rocks around him, heading for the cut and the horses.

Stillman triggered a shot at a skinny man in a leather hat and frock coat retreating through shrubs. Then he jacked another shell and planted a bead on the tall man.

The skinny man bounded toward the old Confederate from behind a tree as Stillman squeezed off his shot.

"Come on, Pap! They're savvy to us!"

The tall man turned to the skinny man, then suddenly grabbed his arm and stumbled back and sideways.

The skinny kid in the leather hat grabbed the older man's arm and tugged as he continued retreating toward the cut.

"You're hit, Pap. Run!"

The older man jerked loose of the kid's grip, straightened, turned defiantly toward Stillman, and raised the big Sharps to his wounded shoulder. Stillman shot at him again, but inadvertently pulled the shot wide. Ignoring the

slug that must have buzzed just past his cheek like a hornet
on the prod, the big man extended his Sharps.

It puffed black smoke and roared.

Stillman ducked back behind his cover, feeling the
boulder shudder as the heavy round smashed into it, throwing shards high in the air. The fragments rained down as
Stillman edged a look around the boulder and saw the old
Confederate, Sharps in one hand and holding his wounded
shoulder with the other, jog away through the rocks and
shrubs toward the cut. The saber swung against his leg.

Stillman snugged the Henry's stock to his cheek, then
lowered the barrel. All the drygulchers were out of range.

He turned left and saw Fred Miller sprawled on his
side along the base of a rock, the Spencer lying across his
left ankle. The old jehu held a hand to his bloody temple
and stretched his lips back from his teeth, in pain. His
weathered face was pale beneath the leathery tan and
birthmark.

Stillman grabbed his hat, scrambled up to the old driver,
and squatted beside him. "Miller, you hit?"

The jehu's voice was thin. "Ricochet, I think."

"Take your hand away, let me see."

The bullet had raked across the oldster's right temple,
digging a small furrow. It was bloody, but Stillman didn't
think the man's skull was cracked. The impact had probably rattled his brain around, however.

Stillman removed his neckerchief and tied it around the
wound. Miller needed more of a bandage than that, but it
would have to do for now.

"Fred, can you stand?"

Miller's eyelids fluttered and he lifted a weak hand toward the sheriff. "Th-think so."

Pulling gently on the man's right arm, Stillman gently
lifted the man to his feet.

"Here, take your Spencer," he said. Miller grabbed the
gun weakly, letting the barrel nudge the ground. Stillman

didn't want to leave it. Before they got to the Rock Creek Station, they might need all the guns they could get.

Stillman swung the arm over his shoulder and, with his other hand around the slender oldster's waist and also holding his Henry, eased Miller down the hill, stepping carefully around rocks and shrubs. Stillman kept his eyes peeled on the west, hoping like hell the gang didn't return.

Miller groused and groaned, panting against the pain. At one point, the old man's foot caught a shrub and the two men nearly went down.

At the base of the hill, on the hill side of the creek, Stillman sat the old man down on a rock and leaned him back against a tree.

"I'm gonna hoof it back for the stage, Fred. Try to stay awake, you hear?"

Miller nodded.

Grasping his Henry in his right hand, Stillman forded the creek and tramped south along the trail, jogging a ways, then walking fast. Not quite fifteen minutes after he'd started, he rounded a bend and saw Evans and Hicks standing in the trail.

"Ben, what happened?" Evans asked.

"We heard the shootin'," Hicks said. "Where's Fred?"

Stillman jogged past them, heading for the stage. "Load up," he ordered the group gathered in the shade, waiting. Fay's eyes snapped wide when she saw him.

Stillman ran to the lead horses tied in the aspen shade, his heart tattooing his breastbone.

He'd run the ambushers off . . . but for how long?

They had to retrieve Miller and split the wind.

4

ROCK CREEK STATION sat in a fold in the dry, brown hills thirty miles north of Sulfur. The motley collection of gray log buildings and corrals straddled the wagon trace, the windmill rattling and clanking in the prairie breeze.

Stillman had wanted to turn back for the safety of Sulfur, but Evans had insisted they continue to Rock Creek, only five or so miles farther north. According to Evans, the jarring stage ride would be excruciatingly painful for Miller, and his wound needed stitching before he bled dry.

The Concord pulled up to the log, sod-roofed cabin built into a hillside, and Gilbert Hicks reined the team to a halt. Stillman sat in the shotgun messenger's seat, Hicks's long-barreled two-bore in his hands. Miller rode in the carriage with the passengers.

Climbing down from the driver's box, Stillman saw two beefy young men in overalls and low-heeled boots lounging on the porch. The one with sandy curly hair was whittling a cottonwood stick, a brown beer bottle near his feet.

Tipped back in his chair, he looked up with mild interest, revealing a blunt face and stupid eyes.

A short, wiry man with mean, close-set eyes and a white goat's beard stepped from the cabin onto the front porch, a scowl pinching his sunburned face as he thumbed his suspenders over his shoulders. He wore a tattered bowler with a chicken feather poking from the leather band. Tufts of gray hair curled from under the hat.

"What happened?" he barked, immediately sensing trouble. The stage's tardiness hadn't overly worried the stationmaster; Pico Place's bleary eyes and wrinkled collar told Stillman he'd been napping.

Quickly, Stillman told the man about the ambush he and Miller had foiled, then opened the stage door. When the women and Judge Bannon had stepped out into the yard, Stillman and Evans led Miller from the stage.

"Miller's not going to be able to ride till tomorrow morning, at least," Stillman told Place.

"He has to," Place snapped. "He's got a timetable to keep, and I ain't set up for overnighters."

Stillman had never liked the crotchety stationmaster, whom he and other lawmen had had to discourage several times, with threat of arrest, from trading whiskey to the down-at-heel Chippewa and Cree who frequently wandered through the area.

"*Get* set up," Stillman told the man as he and Evans guided the jehu up the porch steps. The other passengers milled behind them, stretching and dusting themselves off, glancing around warily.

The stationmaster opened his mouth to object, and Evans cut him off as he snapped the squeaky screen door open. "Place, this man can't ride another mile in his condition. That bullet cut a quarter-inch groove along his skull, and he needs at least one good night's sleep to keep his brain from swelling. I'll have to stick around to keep an eye on him."

"Pshaw!" Place said, regarding Miller walking between

Stillman and Evans, his arms draped over their shoulders. "I been hit worse than that by hail!"

Casting each other wry glances, the sheriff and the doctor led the driver through the cramped cabin's main room, dominated by two plank tables and a giant black range, and into the sleeping area in a lean-to addition off the cabin's north side. When they'd eased Miller onto a cot, Katherine entered the room carrying Evans's black medical kit.

Since the two usually got along when they had to, Stillman headed back outside, where Place's beefy sons were off-hitching the team, fumbling with the buckles and straps, while the passengers stood around, unsure what to do with themselves.

"Sheriff," Mrs. Bannon said, turning her round face with its arched brows from her husband. "*Must* we spend the night at this godforsaken place?"

"Hey, lady!" Place said. He'd been supervising and berating his sons, who in spite of having been hostling teams for the line since they were old enough to feed themselves, still appeared mildly baffled by the harness and leather rigging.

"I'm sorry, Mr. Place, but the soup and sandwiches you served when we came through here a few days ago were nearly inedible. I assume your sleeping accommodations will be little better."

"Prudence," Bannon admonished her gently, patting the gloved hand she had hooked through his elbow. Fay and Crystal stood side by side, between the Bannons and Stillman.

"I told him to keep pullin'," Place said, inclining his head to indicate Stillman. "But he won't hear it. Think I want you all here? Hell, I ain't set up for overnighters!"

Judge Bannon flushed angrily. "Mr. Place, I'll thank you not using gutter talk in front of my wife."

The beefiest of Place's two sons snickered as he led the two lead horses toward the barn.

"This is my station, damn ye," Place intoned, shuttling his gaze to the judge and screwing up his eyes demonically. "If you don't like how—"

"All right!" Stillman said, throwing up his hands. "Everyone settle down. I'm sorry, Mrs. Bannon, but we have to stay the night for Fred Miller's sake. He can't ride in his condition, and he needs Doc Evans' attention."

She narrowed her eyes and opened her mouth to speak, but was stopped suddenly by Stillman's uncompromising gaze. She glanced at her husband as if for help. The judge glanced at Stillman, winced, and looked away.

"Well!" Mrs. Bannon gave a disgusted chuff and looked away, as well.

When the women had gone inside for the midday meal, Stillman and Bannon strolled across the yard.

"Who in the hell were they, Ben?" Bannon asked him. "You have any idea?"

"I couldn't tell," Stillman said. "There's a chance they're after you."

Bannon stopped and turned to him. "Me?"

"At first I thought they were out to clean *my* clock. But when I asked them what they were after, they told me to stay out of it. That was just before they started throwing lead at me and Miller."

"Told you to stay out of it?"

"That's how they put it. Tells me they're after something or some*one* besides myself."

Bannon scrubbed his mottled cheek with a meaty paw, furrowing his silver-gray eyebrows. "Yes, it does, indeed." He glanced at his wife, still standing on the porch, and lowered his voice. "And if not you, more than likely, me . . ."

"That's how I see it. Which means we both have to watch ourselves. We're probably safe here at the station, but we could get hit again tomorrow."

Bannon thought it over, then took a deep breath and regarded Stillman with confidence in his rheumy, blue eyes.

"Well, don't worry about me, Ben." The judge reached inside his coat and produced a revolver from a soft, black shoulder holster hanging under his left arm. He hefted the gun—a silver-plated, pearl-gripped, short-barreled Colt Lightning—in his right hand, and spun the cylinder. "I may spend most of my time behind the bench, but I practice with this little doll in my backyard every Saturday morning. This is one jurist who can watch his own backside."

Bannon offered a confident wink, holstered the Colt, and headed back to the cabin.

Stillman was standing there, staring back the way they'd come, looking for any sign of the desperadoes, when he heard the screen door slap shut behind him. He turned to see Fay walk toward him, her doeskin traveling dress swishing about her long legs, black hair billowing back in the breeze, a tin cup in her hand.

"Coffee?" she said.

"Thanks." He took the coffee and kissed her cheek. "How's everything inside?"

Fay shrugged and fingered a lock of hair back from her face. "Crystal's as chipper as ever, helping Mr. Place make his infamous sandwiches. Katherine's keeping busy, too, helping the doctor with Mr. Miller. I haven't heard any shouting, so maybe they've buried the hatchet. You saw Mrs. Bannon."

"Try to keep her calm, will you?"

"I'll try." Fay followed her husband's gaze south. "Who were they, Ben? What do they want?"

"At first I thought they were after me—"

"Like the men in the Continental?"

Stillman turned his surprised gaze to her.

"I heard the shots. Then, when you and the doc appeared looking sheepish as collie dogs with bellies full of fresh pullet, I put it together. You didn't marry an idjit."

"No, I reckon I didn't," Stillman said, a smile failing amidst his worry. "Anyway, as I was saying, at first I thought they were after me, but now I'm thinking it might be the judge they're after, for some sentence he handed down. He's the only other one I can think of, unless . . ."

"Unless it's us," Fay said simply, finishing the sentence for him. "Us women."

After a moment, Stillman shook his head. "Those boys had murder on their minds, though. They were out for blood, not fun."

"Do you think you discouraged them?"

"Hope so." His tone betrayed his skepticism.

Fay ran her hand across his shoulder, absently brushed at the trail dust collected there, then started back toward the cabin.

"How you feelin'?" Stillman called after her. She was only nine weeks pregnant, but he couldn't help doting. He hadn't wanted her to make the stage ride, but Fay was nothing if not iron-willed. Before learning she was with child, she'd ridden her black Thoroughbred, Dorothy, every morning in the Two-Bear Mountains before heading off to teach in Clantick's one-room school.

Fay turned back to him, her expression level. "Tough enough to eat the devil with his horns on." Her slight French accent—her parents, both from France, had ranched down along the Powder River—added to her expression an exotic sexiness.

The corners of her full mouth rose slightly before she turned and continued toward the cabin.

Stillman turned his gaze again southward, where the pale wagon trace curved through the sage flat and climbed into the distant, pine-covered hills.

They were out there. He didn't know why, but they were.

He could smell the coming trouble like the brimstone of a fast-moving storm.

The gunfire from the botched ambush still echoed in Angus Whateley's ears as, holding his grazed left shoulder with his gloved right hand, he rode his copper-bay stallion into the coulee and reined up before the other members of his family. Quinn rode up behind him and checked his buttermilk down near Angus's left stirrup.

The six men and Temple were gathered in a tight bunch around Skeeter Whateley. Skeeter had apparently been wounded. The skinny kid in a green derby and shabby wool vest slouched over his saddle horn, pressing his right hand against his upper left chest. His shoulders bobbed as he sobbed and spit blood.

"I'm dyin, Pap," he wailed, lifting his skinny, pale face. "I'm dyin'!"

Angus's brother, Cole, sat his own horse beside his son's. He scowled down at the boy with concern. "No, son—I wouldn't go so far as to say you're *dyin'*." He looked at Angus, who was too furious about the ambush to feel sympathy for his nephew's condition. Skeeter had been a whining little troublemaker since he was tit-high to a sow.

"He's hit bad, Angus," Cole Whateley said. His gray eyes were dark and ridged. A bullet or rock shards had cut the knob of his right cheek, and a small ribbon of blood ran into his beard.

Ignoring his brother and his wounded nephew, Angus swept his gaze across the dusty, sweaty group before him. His nostrils flared as the fires of rage seared his loins and climbed his spine. "You ran! Y'all ran like cowardly dogs from a back-alley fracas!"

Cole peered at his older brother and swallowed, always wary of Angus's wrath, which he'd displayed with such murderous force and abandon in Lawrence, Kansas, back in '63. "I wouldn't call it runnin'. We had to retreat, Angus. They got around behind us, took the higher ground."

"Hell, Uncle Angus," Terry Whateley said, sitting to his father's right. He poked his dusty hat back off his pimply forehead. "They were shootin' down at us like ducks on a mill pond. We had to get outta there!"

Quinn heeled his horse forward a step and peered into his father's fiery blue eyes under the heavy, silver brows. Many of the knotted scars on his cheeks and nose he'd acquired while riding with Quantrill and Bloody Bill Anderson during the border wars.

"They're right, Pap," Quinn said. We'll get that judge later. Right now, both you and Skeeter need tendin'."

"We got no time for tendin'." With a distasteful expression, Angus peered at his wounded nephew, whose shoulders bobbed as pain wracked the boy's body. "We gotta ride, son. This ain't no time for tears."

As if to answer his uncle's question, Skeeter groaned. His eyes fluttered as he slid down the side of his saddle and hit the ground on his shoulder and hip. His horse jerked, running into Temple's dun mare. The mute girl in a shapeless homespun frock and man's striped shirt paid little attention to it. Stonily, she glanced down at her suffering cousin. Behind the dirt and sweat on her heart-shaped face, which some called pretty despite a high forehead and a scarred upper lip, she looked bored and distracted.

"Oh, for chrissake!" Angus Whateley snarled.

One hand adjusting the long cavalry saber sheathed on his right side, behind his pistol, he stepped down from his saddle and crouched over Skeeter. Cole Whateley had already dismounted and had dropped to one knee beside his boy. Cole gently pulled the boy's hand away from the wound. He grimaced at the blood, which oozed with every breath.

"Lung-shot," Cole wheezed. He scrubbed his jaw and shook his head.

As if awaiting a judge's decision, the others sat their mounts silently as Angus Whateley lowered his head for a closer look at the wound. When he straightened, his features set and hard, several of the others sighed as well, and shared dark glances.

"He ain't gonna make it," Angus said, turning his gaze to his stocky, bearded brother.

"Maybe there's a doctor back to Sulfur," Cole said half-heartedly, keeping his gaze on the suffering Skeeter.

Angus shook his head. "He won't make it that far. 'Sides, there ain't time. I wanna run that stage down and have that judge swingin' from a tall tree before sunset."

There was a silent pause. The breeze raked the clumps of sage and cedar. The horses snorted and kicked or languidly tore at the grama.

Skeeter's brothers, cousins, and his other uncle, T. L. Brindle—who was married to Cole's middle sister, Claudelle—stared sullenly down at the jerking, crying boy. Having grown up in postwar Missouri, none were given to strong emotion—other than anger, that is. They'd seen their own people die and knew they'd see more. It was a cold fact of their lives.

Angus sighed. "No use lettin' him suffer, Cole. Wouldn't put a deer through it, shouldn't put your boy through it."

Cole looked at him, apprehension glistening in his eyes. His gaze narrowed slightly. "Angus, he's . . . you know he's the apple of his mama's *eye* . . ."

"That's why you shouldn't let him lay here in pain, when he's gonna die one way or the other," Angus said. With a nod toward sympathy and respect for the situation, he kept his voice low but placed his hand on the walnut grips of his Remington .44. "Now, you gonna do it or should I?"

The boy was sobbing with his face in the grass, gently bending his knees as if trying to run. He glanced up at Angus, terror in his eyes. He opened his mouth to speak, and blood frothed over his lips.

"I'll do it, if you want, Pap," said Sammy Whateley, Cole's oldest. "Me an' Skeeter, we never did get along for beans, anyhow."

Temple turned to him and tugged on his arm, grunting.

"Temple said she'd do it," Sammy said. "You know how she is with a gun. She'd make it so he wouldn't feel a thing."

Temple turned to her uncle Cole and smiled, nodding.

"Shut up!" Cole raged, climbing to his feet. "Skeeter's the apple of his mama's eye, and this has gotta be done right!"

Punctuating his sentence, a pistol popped. Cole jumped back with a start and looked down. A small round hole in the back of Skeeter's head, just behind the boy's right ear, trickled blood. The boy sighed and lay still.

Angus stood over him, long-barreled Colt extended in his right hand. Smoke licked from the barrel.

Angus holstered the pistol and turned to Cole, his eyes brightly impatient. " 'Nuff o' this nonsense. Time to turn the coons loose on that stage!"

5

THREE HOURS AFTER the stage had reached the station, Doc Evans checked on Fred Miller again. Finding the man sound asleep and the stitches holding fast, Evans strolled out to the cabin's front porch.

He closed the door quietly behind him, so as not to wake the judge and Mrs. Bannon, who were napping while Fay and Crystal worked in the cabin's kitchen area, preparing supper. He reached for the whiskey flask in his back pocket.

Noticing someone sitting on the porch to his left, he stopped his hand's movement and turned to see Katherine. She sat in a scroll-back chair on the other side of a rain barrel and rusty tin washtub, staring absently into the distance. She'd removed her feathered hat, but she'd left her auburn hair in its neat, fist-sized bun.

"Go ahead and swill your snake water, Clyde," she said, not turning to him. "Don't mind me."

An angry flush began inching up the back of his neck, but was dissipated quickly by contrition. Katherine had helped him suture Miller's head. Something about their closeness in the sleeping room and how secure he'd felt working beside her had made him regret last night's bad behavior.

Something about Katherine Kemmett always brought out the very best and the very worst in him. Before Katherine, no single person, let alone a woman, had ever frustrated him to the point of his wanting to cut his own head off with a rusty saw. But at the moment, he was only frustrated with himself, and remorseful.

He stepped to the edge of the porch, placed a hand on an awning post, and cast his gaze about the yard in which the afternoon shadows had gathered. Pico Place's lazy, beefy sons played checkers on a fruit crate outside the main corral while Gilbert Hicks replaced a hinge on the corral's rear gate.

"Where's Ben?" Evans asked conversationally.

"Last I saw, he and Mr. Place were walking out behind the barn."

Evans dropped his chin and toed a loose board with a scuffed brogan. "Thanks for helping with Fred."

"It's my job."

Evans sighed. He deserved this coolness. After a bit, he cleared his throat, tongued his cheek, and stared unseeing at the barn across the yard.

He took a deep breath and steeled himself. "Katherine, I'm sorry about last night. I was out of line, and I behaved very badly."

He was hoping that she would forgive him so that he could forgive himself and they could go back to being at least civil to one another, but she said nothing. She sat in her chair without speaking or moving, just staring at a wooded hill behind the barn. Along the hill, two figures moved, one carrying a rifle. That would be Ben and Pico Place.

Finally, Evans turned to Katherine. "Did you hear me? I said I was sorry."

Crisply, she said, "I heard you, Clyde."

"Well, do you forgive me?"

She turned her head to him, her eyes flinty, lips pursed. "It was very embarrassing, what you did. The entire hotel heard it. What they must think about us . . . about me."

He knew she was remembering the night they'd spent together, in the house she'd once shared with her husband, the late Reverend Kemmett, nearly twenty years her senior. She was so guilt-ridden about that night that they'd never repeated it. In fact, though he knew she'd enjoyed it as much as he had, she'd become annoyingly coy and distant. And he could tell by her demeanor that she was worried now that Evans had given away their shameful secret.

Keeping his voice level, Evans said, "Katherine, I'm trying to apologize."

"You did apologize, Clyde. What happened last night—had you gambled all your money away and couldn't afford the pleasures of Sulfur's professional women?"

She instantly regretted saying it, for the look that crept into his eyes was one she'd rarely seen in Clyde Evans's eyes before. Genuine hurt. For an instant, the doctor appeared totally without his customary guile. It was a fleeting look that he fought off a second later with a lascivious arch of his right brow and an upward quirk of his thick, red mustache.

Feigning indifference, and embarrassed by the vulnerability he'd accidentally let show, if only for a moment, he chuckled dryly, plucked a cheroot from his vest pocket, and walked down into the yard as he fished a match from his pants.

Katherine watched him, frowning at his back as, blue cigar smoke billowing about his head, he ducked through the corral fence and disappeared around the barn. She wanted to call out to him, to tell him that she did forgive him, but for some reason she couldn't summon the words.

Whether it was directed at him or herself, her anger and frustration flared. She balled the hands in her lap into fists, squeezed her eyes shut, and muttered beneath her breath, *"Clyde Evans!"*

His remorse was now gone, replaced with anger—a more comfortable emotion, anyway. *Thank you, Katherine, you sad, inhibited bitch.* Evans puffed the cigar with vigor as he climbed the hill behind the barn. He found Ben and Pico Place at the bald knob of the hill. Stillman directed a field glass southward while Place stood nearby, holding a beer bottle and chewing a wild oat stem, hands in the pockets of his checked, threadbare trousers, fidgeting.

"Any sign of them?" Evans asked.

Stillman shook his head as he swept the glass slowly from left to right. "Nothing. But I keep getting the feeling we're being watched."

"I had a friend like that," Place said, snickering and breaking wind. "Hunted buffalo with him years ago. He couldn't stand it out here, kept imagining folks starin' at him from behind every knob and . . ." He let the thought dance off, picked up another. "Course he did get scalped by the Kiowa. And the Cheyenne, hell, they gave him a time, too!"

Stillman lowered the glass and turned to the station manager. "Place, how well are you and your sons armed?"

The man shrugged and acquired a piqued look. "We can defend ourselves."

"How many rifles?"

"We each got a long gun, and I keep a shotgun in the kitchen. Double-barrel Greener I won off 'n a—"

"Plenty of ammo?"

Place frowned up at Stillman, who had a good five inches on the man. "You don't really think they're gonna attack the station, do ye?"

"Place, I've got four women down there, and I don't intend to let anything happen to them. We were attacked once, we could be attacked again . . . anytime, anywhere. We men will take turns keeping watch all night. Now, I suggest you head back to the cabin. You and your boys clean and ready your weapons."

Place stared up at Stillman, anger entering his pinched gaze. He licked his dry lips and tugged on his white goat beard. With a cautious, slightly beseeching air, he said, "Now, listen here, I don't cotton to bein' ordered around my own station. Not even by the likes o' you, Mr. Stillman . . ."

"I don't care what you like, Place. I'm the man with the most experience in these situations. What I say goes. Another thing I'm going to tell you, and I'll only tell you once—you and your boys stay away from that beer of yours. I smell it on your breath anymore between now and tomorrow morning, I'm gonna pour out that whole tub you have working in your smithy shed. Understand?"

"You can't—!"

"Understand, Mr. Place?" Stillman's voice was taut as Glidden wire.

Place chuffed, gave his beard another tug. "I reckon I ain't got no choice."

"Now get down there and see if the women need help fixing supper. We could all use a *good,* hot meal."

When Place had gone, cursing and snarling, Evans removed the cigar from his mouth and studied the white coal. "Never did like that man. Wonder why the line ever hired him."

Evans watched the sheriff. Stillman was again surveying the distance through the field lens.

"You really think we're being watched?" Evans asked.

"I don't know," the lawman said. "Maybe I'm jumping at hoot owls, but I have a few hairs standing up straight on the back of my neck. Those hairs saved my hide a few times, so I think I'll stick with 'em." He glanced at Evans smoking beside him. "How's Fred?"

"I did my usual artful suturing job. If he gets a good night's sleep, I don't see why he won't be able to ride again in the morning. That isn't to say, however, that he won't feel like he painted his tonsils with a couple tubs of Mr. Place's tornado juice."

"How's Katherine?"

Evans turned to the sheriff and narrowed his eyes behind his glinting spectacles. "Huh?"

"Still mad?" Stillman half-smiled.

Evans looked away and shrugged. "That woman was born mad. She'll die mad."

Stillman reduced the lens between his palms. "Leave her be, Doc. Give her some time. Then, if she sees any good in you at all, she'll come around."

He stuck the field lens inside his coat, picked up his rifle, and started down the hill.

"What if there *ain't* any good in me?" Evans called after him.

It sounded like a serious question.

Stillman turned and looked back up the hill, a wry smile lifting the corners of his salt-and-pepper mustache. "Then neither one of you has anything to worry about."

He started down the hill again, calling over his shoulder, "Come on—it ain't safe out here alone."

An hour later, sitting at one of the cabin's two eating tables, Stillman wiped his mustache with a piece of yellowed newspaper and slid his plate away. "That was good stew," he told Crystal and Fay. Crystal was pouring coffee for Pico Place while Fay sponged off the food-preparation table beside the range.

Crystal gave Stillman a wink. "Amazing what can be done with a few airtights and wrinkled-up potatoes. But don't blame me and Fay if you get a bellyache later. Some of those tins looked like they'd been gathering dust since before the Alamo."

Place looked the girl up and down, grinning. "Who-eeee—sure is nice havin' ladies around to cook and clean up the place." He glanced at his two sons eating alone at the other table. Larry and Norman hunkered over their plates, shoveling stew into their mouths as though they hadn't eaten in weeks. "Ain't it, boys?"

"Sure is, Pap," said Larry, the younger, as he raised his bowl to his mouth and shoveled the stew with his spoon, not missing a drop.

"Yeah, sure is," allowed Norman, dropping his spoon in his empty bowl, belching loudly, and regarding Crystal's shapely backside with a grin as the blonde poured coffee for Gilbert Hicks.

Stillman felt a father's protectiveness toward Crystal, since she'd married his best friend's son and Stillman was her child's godfather, but he controlled his anger. Norman Place's experience with women was probably limited to the few ladies who passed through the station each month. Seeing women as pretty as Fay and Crystal was no doubt a rare treat.

What really knotted Stillman's tail was the way their father, Place, kept ogling Fay, like he was doing now.

"No more coffee for me," Stillman told Crystal as he grabbed his Henry from the wall beside him, snapped it to his shoulder, and aimed the barrel at Place's head.

The stationmaster jerked back on the bench and crossed his hands before his face. "No! Sheriff, don't!"

"You been drinkin' again, Place?"

"N-no, I ain't had a drop since you told me not to!"

"Just checking," Stillman said, lowering the Henry to his side.

All eyes had turned to him. Place's boys had frozen,

jaws dropping, eyes wide as saucers. Crystal snickered, Evans chuckled, and Fay said, "Ben, good grief . . ."

Pico Place let out a little warble of relief as he lowered his arms and broke wind.

"It's getting dark," Stillman said, glancing out the front windows as he stood. "I'll take the first watch on the hill behind the barn. Two hours apiece ought to get us through the night. Gil, you'll take the second watch."

Prudence Bannon placed a hand on her husband's arm and frowned at Stillman. She said quietly, "Why are you making all the decisions around here, Sheriff? Doesn't my husband, being a circuit judge, outrank you?"

"Now, Prudence," Bannon said, smiling and flushing, patting the hand she'd placed on his arm. "I defer entirely to Ben here. He's been in many similar situations, and it would be downright silly of me to do anything less. We all must do as he says."

The judge glanced at Stillman, who stood with one foot on the bench he'd been sitting on. "Ben, I'll take a turn on guard duty, like everyone else."

Stillman shook his head. "Too risky, Judge. I'm afraid it's you those men are after. You and your wife stay inside as much as possible."

Prudence Bannon flushed, annoyed by another order, but said nothing as she lowered her eyes to her stew, which she'd hardly touched.

Stillman turned to the station agent. "Place, you'll take the watch after Gil. Then Larry and Norman here. You boys stay together, keep each other awake."

"I don't want to sit up in the dark," Norman said. "I work hard around here; I need my shut—"

Stillman shook his head and furrowed his brows, having none of it. "Don't let me catch either of you sawin' wood, hear?"

"What about the doc?" Place said, indignant.

"He's gotta keep an eye on Fred."

Place was about to object, but Stillman waved him off.
"Shh!"

They all listened. The clomp of hooves rose in the
southern distance.

"Horses!" Bannon hissed.

Stillman rushed to the door, threw it open, and stepped
onto the porch as he jacked a shell into the Henry's breech.

"Identify yourselves!" he yelled back along the trail.
The land was darkening fast while the sky was emerald
green. Shadows moved about fifty yards from the edge of
the station yard. A bit chain rattled.

"Ralph and Tim Dooley!" a man yelled. Stillman noted
a slight Southern accent. "We mean no harm. Just driftin',
that's all."

There was a pause.

Stillman turned to the station agent, who'd stepped out
onto the porch. "Heard of 'em?"

Place shook his head.

The voice rose again. "Can we come in?"

"Ride in slow," Stillman ordered as he stepped into the
middle of the yard, his rifle raised to port. Boots thumped
on the porch, and he half-turned to see Gil Hicks's bulky
silhouette and the shorter one of Doc Evans. Bannon stood
in the doorway.

"Gil, Doc," Stillman said, "watch my back, will you?
This could be a trick."

"You got it, Sheriff," Hicks said. Stillman heard the rasp
of a shell being levered into a rifle breech. Hicks stepped
down off the porch and moved to the cabin's north side,
staying within the low-slung building's shadows.

Evans muttered something; then the door clicked shut,
reducing the light in the yard. Stillman peered into the
darkness ahead of him, watched the silhouettes of two
horseback riders shape themselves against the twilight sky.

"That's far enough," Stillman said. The two riders
halted their horses twenty yards away.

One of the horses blew and shook its head.

"Come in slow," Stillman said.

"I'm Ralph Dooley, and this is my brother, Tim. We seen the lights and wondered if we could get a hot cup of coffee, possibly something to eat. We've been on the trail a few days."

"We can pay for it, of course," the other man said.

"Where you Dooleys from and where you headed?" Stillman normally put such inquiries less directly; snooping wasn't the frontier way. But under the circumstances, he didn't care whom he offended. That attempted bushwhacking had offended him plenty.

"We're from down Colorady way, and we're headin' to the gold fields up in Cany-da," said Ralph.

"Got tired of brush-poppin' herd-quitters, we did," added Tim. "Now, we're lookin' to see some real money for a hell of a lot less work."

While listening to the night for any suspicious sounds, Stillman sized up the two men before him. In their early twenties, they wore a few days' growth of beard and grubby range clothes. One of them was even wearing brush-scarred batwing chaps. Their horses stood hangheaded, tired.

The only weapons Stillman could see were the two old carbines jutting from their saddle boots.

"You boys traveling without six-shooters?"

Ralph glanced at Tim, then turned to Stillman. "They're in our saddlebags. We don't carry 'em less'n we're countin' on trouble." He gave Stillman a sidelong look. "There ain't no trouble here, is there, mister?"

"Not at the moment," Stillman said. He paused, squeezing the Henry when a night bird flew low across the yard, wings making a sinewy flapping sound.

Stillman eased his grip on the rifle and continued. "Our stage was attacked earlier, so I'm not takin' any chances with you two. For all I know, you're ridin' for the gang that attacked us."

Tim raised his gloved hands from his saddle horn, but before he could speak, Stillman said, "I apologize for the prickly welcome, but if you boys want to stay here, you'll bed down in the barn. I or one of the other men will bring out some food and coffee. Lights out in an hour. Don't let me catch you lurkin' around tonight, understand?"

The two strangers exchanged enigmatic glances. Even in the thickening shadows, the looks were not lost on Stillman, who stepped aside to let them pass.

"It sure *ain't* a warm welcome," Tim huffed.

Ralph gave Tim a harsh look, but spoke to Stillman. "We understand—don't we, Tim? In this godforsaken country, you can't be too careful. The barn's just fine. Just fine," he added as he nudged his horse forward.

His brother followed suit, and the two men walked their horses past Stillman. The lawman watched as the men dismounted before the barn. Handing his reins to Tim, Ralph lifted the bar and swung the barn doors wide.

"There's a lamp on a post to your right," Pico Place yelled from the porch. "Careful—it's got a leak. Don't burn my barn down!"

Neither man responded as they led their mounts up the ramp and into the barn's inner darkness.

"What do you think?" Evans said, stepping up beside Stillman.

"They might be who say they are," Stillman allowed. "But the man in the canyon had a drawl like theirs."

"A lot of men in the West have drawls like theirs."

Stillman nodded as he stared at the barn. A lantern mantle squeaked and a dull glow appeared in the cracks between the barn's unchinked logs. "If we get through the night without trouble, I'll smoke the peace pipe with 'em in the morning. But I've been gopherin' in these hills since

Sitting Bull was a calf, and I don't need tumbleweeds to tell me which way the wind is blowing."

Evans stared at him. "Cut the deck a little deeper for me, will you?"

Stillman stared at the lantern's glow between the cracks in the barn wall, then glanced at Evans before turning and heading for the cabin. "I'm gonna keep an eye on 'em."

6

PRUDENCE BANNON LAY in the darkness of the women's area of the sleeping room, and tapped her fingers silently on the wooden cot frame. She and the other women had retired more than an hour ago, and Prudence could tell by the deep, measured breaths around her that she was the only one who hadn't yet fallen asleep.

It wasn't the men's snoring on the other side of the curtain, the discomfort of the old Army cot, or the scratchy wool blanket that kept her awake. It wasn't fear of the renegades who'd attempted to ambush the stage, either.

It was the look in the eyes of Dr. Clyde Evans when, on the ride out here from the north, the doctor had remembered where he'd seen her before. She could tell the doctor had been trying to place her since she and the judge had boarded in Chinook. Fortunately, Evans's own spotted history had prevented him from inquiring aloud.

When she and her husband had first moved to Montana's Hi-Line after they'd been married in Leadville, Colorado

Territory, she'd learned that Evans was one of only two doctors in the area. For the past two years, she'd been avoiding the doctor, which wasn't too difficult since she and her husband lived in Chinook, twenty miles east of Clantick. The less Evans saw her, she figured, the less the chance of his remembering their first meeting in the mining camps around Billings during a humbler time in her life, and possibly mentioning that meeting to John.

How horrified she'd been to see him on the stage, and then to see the fleeting look of recognition in his eyes!

The judge had known her only as a singer and dancer for wealthy cattlemen and railroad moguls in the Montana House in Billings and in a few opera houses in Deadwood and Cheyenne. If the judge knew what she'd done before that—been forced to do by circumstances beyond her control—she wasn't sure how he would react.

But she had an idea. At twenty-nine, she was too old for the more refined dance halls in the larger settlements, so she'd be forced to return to the mining camps to earn a living.

Damn that Evans!

The thought caused cold sweat beads to pop out on her upper lip, and before she knew it, she'd thrown back the crusty wool blanket and swung her feet to the floor. Having removed only her expensive, Turkish boots, she stepped into them now and carelessly tied the silk laces.

Rising, feeling her heart hammering in her chest, she wove her way between the cots where the other ladies slept, and gently swept the blanket curtain aside. She let the blankets fall back into place and moved quickly across the cabin, careful not to kick a chair or a table leg.

Quietly, she lifted the front door's locking bar, opened the door, and stepped out onto the porch.

She latched the door behind her, then stepped to the edge of the porch and crossed her arms over her breasts. She took a deep, calming breath and suppressed a shudder as the images of those mining camps—drunken miners, close-range pistol fights, diseased curs running wild—reeled through her head like tintypes on caroming pinwheels.

She didn't know how long she'd been standing there, staring into the star-shrouded night, when the door latch clicked. She turned with a start. John stepped through the open door, wearing his coat over his shirt, which he had not bothered to tuck into his pants. His eyes were puffy, and his hair was mussed from sleep.

He frowned at her and said softly, "Prudence? I thought I heard someone. What in blazes—?"

"It was so stuffy in there, I couldn't sleep," she said.

Bannon glanced quickly around, spotting the wagon across the yard, where Place's beefy sons had bedded down. "You shouldn't be out here alone."

"The sheriff's keeping watch," she said, trying to sound as though nothing were bothering her. "I saw no reason to be afraid." At least, not of outlaws. "Besides," she said, stepping slowly toward him and smiling up into his face, "you'll protect me from the badmen, won't you, John?"

Prudence's insecurities had always driven her, and they drove her now to press her breasts against her husband's chest and to wrap her arms around his neck. Her innate charm and ability to evoke desire were tools she'd learned to use on men from very early on.

"Won't you?" she said, rubbing her nose against his cheek and grinning impishly.

Despite himself, Bannon chuckled, took another quick glance around the yard, saw the two inert lumps in the wagon, and wrapped his arms around her waist. She pressed her lips against his, probed his mouth with her tongue. He was reluctant at first, but after a few seconds he opened his mouth wider, ran his hands up her back, pulling her closer, until she could feel the reaction she was waiting for.

She pulled a few inches away and stared into his lust-narrowed eyes. "Wanna be naughty?" she whispered through a smile.

"Here—?" Again, he glanced around.

"Not here, silly," she said, taking his hand and leading him down the porch steps. "This way . . . follow me. . . ."

Jerking on his hand, she led him around behind the cabin to an open shed in which several cords of split wood had been haphazardly stacked. The smell of pine resin was sharp. Some small night critter scuttled from the wood and into the tall grass behind the shed. Several tall cottonwoods blocked the stars, and the darkness was so dense that the judge and Mrs. Bannon had to feel their way in amongst the wood with their hands, treading lightly.

Several times Prudence giggled, and Bannon shushed her. "Prudence, please," the judge admonished, stifling his own chuckles. "I'm a jurist, for Pete's sake! We mustn't be discovered."

"Hurry, John! I feel very, very naughty!"

He brushed his shin on a jutting pine log and cursed under his breath. "This isn't dignified."

"No, it isn't," she tittered.

As she moved toward him and placed her hands on the buttons of his fly, his knees nearly buckled with desire.

Fifteen minutes after the judge had gone out, Clyde Evans's bladder woke him. The doctor considered using the wooden oat bucket that served as a thunder mug, but decided it might wake the women.

As the other men snored away on their cots, he threw on his shirt and trousers, stepped into his shoes, and shuffled through the dark cabin to the door. Outside, he padded around the cabin's south side, making for the single-hole privy sitting out back.

A sound stopped him on the footpath halfway between the cabin and the outhouse. What sounded like a grunt had come from around the woodshed thirty feet left of the privy, under the giant cottonwood whose uppermost leaves rattled in a slight breeze.

Alarm bells tolled in Evans's brain. His back stiffened. As he stood frozen, listening, another sound rose from the wood shed.

This one sounded like a woman's muffled groan.

A dull thud, like a falling log.

A man said, "Shh."

Evans's heart thudded, and his vision swam. One of the women had been nabbed by the gang!

Before he knew it, he was running toward the woodshed crouching blackly against the sky, his feet pounding through the dew-damp brush. Bounding around the corner of the wood pile and glaring into a horseshoe made by the stacked wood, he yelled, "What's going on?"

A woman gave a shrill *"Oh, my God!"*

At the same time, a man's breathy grunt was followed by *"What . . . !"*

Evans blinked into the shadows, horrified to see the judge stumble back from his wife's spread legs, reaching for the pants bunched around his ankles.

"Oh, my—I'm sorry," Evans said, wheeling and bringing a shielding hand to his eyes. "I heard suspicious noises over here, and I thought . . . I thought. . . ." He let it go, gritting his teeth against the image seared into his brain.

Stumbling over fallen logs, Prudence pulled her bloomers up, let her dress fall back around her knees, and ran out from the shed, pummeling Evans with a murderous glare. "You drunken—" She stammered before adding, *"Pervert!"* Then she turned and ran back toward the cabin.

Buttoning his pants, Bannon cast the doctor a similar glare. "You miserable son of a bitch—we'll talk about this tomorrow."

"Judge, I said I was sorry. I thought—"

Bannon stopped. He was far enough away that Evans

could see only his beefy silhouette, not the murderous look the doctor knew was there. "I know what you thought, you drunken fool. You keep your mouth shut about this, you understand?"

Evans felt his face burning in the dark, but he said nothing. So much for helping a damsel in distress. As the judge ran to catch up to his wife, the doctor heard Prudence Bannon say in a pinched voice, "I never . . . !"

Behind them, Evans spit under his breath, "Oh, I think you have, Mrs. Bannon." Chuckling, suddenly feeling as pleased as a schoolboy who'd just humiliated the most pompous girl in class, he turned and stomped off to the privy. "Oh, yes, Mrs. Bannon," he added, remembering a Miss Norma Koslowski from the Soda Butte settlement near Billings, "I think you have, indeed. . . ."

Five minutes later, Ben Stillman walked along the north side of the barn, pleased to hear soft snores issuing from the two Southern strangers who'd bedded down inside. He brushed past the wagon in which one of Place's sons was giggling in his sleep, mumbling, "Ain't you just bein' a goofy girl!" and headed across the station yard toward the cabin.

He paused when he saw two human silhouettes standing near a clump of rabbitbush about ten feet out from the cabin's north wall. Tensing, he raised his rifle. Then he heard Bannon speaking in hushed tones.

"Judge?"

Both figures swung toward Stillman, one gasping.

Stillman walked toward them, his rifle in both hands. "Judge, what are you doing out here?"

"Nothing," Bannon said quickly, sounding a little sheepish. "The missus here was just, uh, startled by Doc Evans on her way to the privy."

"I see," Stillman said. "Tense night, I reckon."

Without saying anything, Prudence Bannon, looking angry in the wan starlight, slipped out of her husband's grasp and brushed past Stillman on her way to the cabin's front door.

Stillman turned to Bannon. "I hope she isn't too upset."

"No," Bannon said. "Like you said . . . just a tense night."

Stillman nodded. He turned to the porch as someone rounded the cabin's far front corner. "Hold it!" Stillman ordered, raising the rifle hip-high.

He recognized Evans's stocky figure. The doctor, as startled as Stillman, stopped suddenly and threw up his hands.

"What the hell's goin' on out here?" Stillman said, lowering the Henry and shuttling his gaze between Evans and Bannon. "A hoedown?"

The judge snorted, gave the doctor a withering look, then quietly disappeared into the cabin.

Stillman turned to Evans, who'd lowered his hands. "Now what'd you do?"

"I took a piss, if that's all right with you and everybody else!" Evans rasped, red-faced with indignation. Shaking his head and heaving an angry sigh, he mounted the porch steps, and disappeared inside.

After Stillman had rousted Gil Hicks for the second watch, the lawman slept fitfully on the hide sofa covered with feed sack cushions for an hour. When Hicks returned to summon Pico Place to the starlit knoll behind the barn, Stillman rose, as well, and patrolled the grounds around the station.

He returned to the cabin and slept again until he woke to Pico Place rousting his sons from their wagon bed. Place shouted at them loud enough to wake everyone, calling them ill-mannered, lazy hounds. He finished by telling them how neither one was fit for civilized company and how he rued the day he'd ever knocked up their worthless, cheating mother.

When Place came in and lay down on his cot near the

other men, instantly rattling the windows with his snores, Stillman snorted, turned onto his side, folded his arms across his chest, and drifted back to sleep. He didn't know how long he'd slept when a muffled scream jolted him awake, his right hand reaching for the Henry leaning against the couch.

He sat up, blinking. Gray light washed through the cracks in the shuttered windows, and morning birds chirped in the branches outside the cabin. He stood before the sofa, listening, hearing only the snoring of the other men in the cabin, wondering if he'd only dreamed the distant scream.

Then it came again. A man's cry.

Stillman bolted to the unbarred door, threw it open, and stepped outside.

"No!" A man's bellow rose from behind the barn, crisp in the quiet morning air. "Oh, ye dirty, mangy dogs!"

It was Pico Place.

Stillman leapt from the porch and sprinted around the barn, his heart thudding wildly. He followed the path through the sage, leapt the creek, and trudged up the side of the hill, weaving through the stunt cedars and sage.

Place's wails grew louder as Stillman ran, breathing hard against the climb. Topping out on the hill's crest, Stillman stopped suddenly, scowling down where Pico Place sat on the grassy ground, his back against a boulder, one hand on the low limb of the cedar to his right, the other on a mossy rock to his left.

He grabbed at the tree and the rock, as though trying to rise but not finding the strength. "No! Oh, no! My boys! My beloved boys!"

Stillman followed Place's gaze to the far side of the hill's crest.

"Holy Christ," he muttered as he took several slow steps forward. His belly filled with acid.

Sitting against a rocky dike twenty yards away were the two Place boys. Bloody stumps where their heads used to be, they sat with their backs against the dike, boots straight out before them. Their clothes were soaked with blood.

In their laps, cradled between their lifeless hands, their heads sat like bloody gourds. The faces stared up at Stillman with bared teeth and slitted, sightless eyes.

Pico Place cried out from deep in his chest. "Oh, you mangy curs—look what you done to my *beautiful* boys!"

7

IN A ROCKY gorge a mile west of the stage station, Angus Whateley sat against his saddle and stared into the fire he'd been tending all night as he drank coffee, chewed jerky, and waited for his son Wayne and his nephew Vernon to return with the judge.

The gang, glassing the station from a hilltop earlier, had determined that the stage was going to remain at the station overnight. Wayne and Vernon had eagerly volunteered to ride into the station under the guise of ordinary cowpokes, and nab the judge in the middle of the night. The boys would sneak him out without firing a shot.

Angus had gone along with the plan, because Wayne and Vernon had been so certain they could pull it off. The two had probably rustled more Kansas beef than anyone else in Missouri, and looked and smelled like bona-fide waddies. And they were damn sneaky. Moreover, Vernon was slick with his old Confederate pistol.

The coffeepot gurgled on a hot rock, and Angus reached over to pour himself another cup.